For Glynis, old pal, and for
Niamh and Eoin, with love.

I AM I

Marie-Louise Fitzpatrick

A NEAL PORTER BOOK
ROARING BROOK PRESS
NEW MILFORD, CONNECTICUT

My mountain is
BIGGEST.

My tree
is
tallest.

Mine is the
beautiful thing.

Mine,
mine,
mine!

Beautiful thing is dead, all gone. I am I and I feel very, very small.

Dead, all gone. I am I and I am sorry.

The main inspiration for this book comes from a Native American river symbol. The Choctaw say
that just as you cannot stand on both sides of a river at once, you cannot belong to two cultures.
But sometimes when the river narrows, the banks come close together and
you can lean out and touch someone on the other side. The symbol looks like this:

Thanks (again) to Diarmuid, Donnchadh and Cian for "being" Skyboy and Earthboy. A month
at Fundación Valparaíso, Mojácar, Spain, helped get this idea going. I found one mountain (La Vieja)
just outside the back door, as well as the dry riverbed and buckets of inspiration.
A year later at the Eleanor Dark Writers Centre at Varuna, Katoomba, Australia I cut through so many
problems and made loads more progress. My stay at Varuna was organized by the Tyrone Guthrie Centre,
Co. Monaghan. Of course I found the second mountain at Kata Tjuta in the Northern Territory. Travel to Spain
and Australia was made possible by a grant from South Dublin County Council.

Many thanks to all the above for these great opportunities to find new
colors, ideas—and mountains! To the lovely people I met at both centres—all the best, always.

—Marie-Louise Fitzpatrick

Copyright © 2006 by Marie-Louise Fitzpatrick
A Neal Porter Book
Published by Roaring Brook Press
Roaring Brook Press is a division of Holtzbrinck Publishing Holdings Limited Partnership
143 West Street, New Milford, Connecticut 06776

Distributed in Canada by H. B. Fenn and Company Ltd.

Library of Congress Cataloging-in-Publication Data
Fitzpatrick, Marie-Louise.
I am I / Marie-Louise Fitzpatrick. — 1st ed.
p. cm. "A Neal Porter book."
Summary: Two small boys wage war against each other in this parable about the futility of fighting.
ISBN-13: 978-1-59643-054-9   ISBN-10: 1-59643-054-0
[1. War—Fiction. 2. Parables.]   I. Title.
PZ7.F585Iae 2006   [E]—dc22   2005016651

Roaring Brook Press books are available for special promotions and premiums.
For details contact: Director of Special Markets, Holtzbrinck Publishers.

Printed in China
First Edition June 2006
2 4 6 8 10 9 7 5 3 1